The AMAZING DAYS of ABBY HAYES

Two Heads Are Better Than One

Read all the books about me!

#1 Every Cloud Has a Silver Lining

#2 The Declaration of Independence

#3 Reach For The Stars

#4 Have Wheels, Will Travel

#5 Look Before You Leap

#6 The Pen is Mightier Than The Sword

#7 Two Heads are Better Than One

#8 The More, The Merrier

#9 Out of Sight, Out of Mind

#10 Everything New Under the Sun

Dear Friends,
Do you like my new look?
I decided it was time for a change.
And that's not the only
new thing that's happening!
Read on to find out more!
Love, Abby

 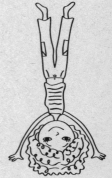

 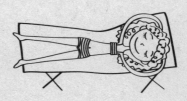

The AMAZING DAYS of ABBY HAYES

Two Heads Are Better Than One

ANNE MAZER

AN
APPLE
PAPERBACK

SCHOLASTIC INC.
New York Toronto London Auckland Sydney
Mexico City New Delhi Hong Kong Buenos Aires

To all the students in the Cortland city school district:
Randall, Smith, Virgil, Barry, and Parker Elementary Schools.
With a special thank-you for an unforgettable birthday
to the students at Virgil and Randall!

ISBN 0-439-35366-1

12 11 10 9 8 7 6   4 5 6 7/0

Printed in the U.S.A.   40

First Scholastic printing, April 2002

Chapter 1

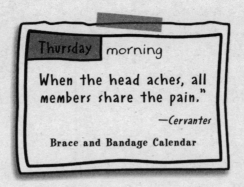

> Thursday morning
>
> When the head aches, all members share the pain."
>
> —Cervantes
>
> **Brace and Bandage Calendar**

Does that mean family members? I wish they'd share my pain. There is plenty to go around. My head aches, my arms ache, my legs ache – even my eyelashes ache!

I have been home with the flu for four days now. It feels like forever!

Advantages of Being Sick:
1. Can watch as much TV as I want.
2. No school or homework.
3. No chores.
4. Sleep all day.
5. Meals in room.

<u>Disadvantages of Being Sick:</u>
1. Too tired to watch TV.
2. Behind on schoolwork.
3. Bored. Achy. Feverish.
4. Crumbs in bed.
5. I miss my friends!

Last week, seven people in our class were out with the flu.

Brianna and Bethany came down with it on the same day. (Bethany <u>always</u> imitates Brianna!)

Mason turned green in the middle of the math quiz. (How did he time that just right?)

Jessica was out for ten days. (My best friend has asthma, which makes every cold or flu worse.)

Natalie was absent for only two days. (My other best friend hardly ever gets sick.)

Zach was so ill he didn't want to play computer games. (Can this be true?)

Ms. Bunder got the flu and had to cancel creative writing class! (Boo-hoo! Ms.

Bunder, why did you get sick last week instead of _this_ week?)

This morning I got out of bed for the first time in days. I went downstairs. Everyone was eating breakfast.

"You look like a ghost," said my older sister Eva. She is too healthy to get the flu. She drinks power shakes and exercises every two minutes.

"Take vitamins," said Eva's twin, Isabel. If Isabel got the flu, she would put it under a microscope and study it. Or write a paper about it. She wouldn't lie in bed and moan.

My little brother, Alex, looked scared when he saw me. "Will Abby have to go to the hospital?" he asked.

I tried to say, "I'm okay," but I croaked like a frog instead.

Help! I am turning into a ghost-frog! No one in my family has the flu except me. They are all at school or work. Dad is

upstairs in his home office. He gave me a bell to ring if I need him. I have a glass of water by the bed and a box of tissues. The TV is in my room but I think I'll go to sleep again...

Abby turned over in bed and looked at the clock. It was three-thirty in the afternoon. She had slept through most of the day again.

Slowly she moved her arms and legs. She felt less achy but she was still congested. When was she going to get better?

The telephone rang. A minute later, a gentle knock sounded at the door.

"Abby? Are you up?" It was Alex.

"Come in, Alex." Abby blew her nose loudly.

"Jessica's on the phone." He handed her the cordless telephone.

"Hi, Jessica," Abby said hoarsely to her best friend.

"How are you?" Jessica said. "We miss you in school!"

Abby lay back on the pillow. "This morning I wrote in my journal for fifteen minutes. Then I slept for the rest of the day!" She coughed. "I miss every-one, too."

"You sound terrible," Jessica said.

"I *am* terrible," Abby agreed. "So terrible that no one will get near me. You should have seen Alex run out of my room just now."

"He doesn't want to get sick," Jessica said. She was always practical.

"It's not fair!" Abby wailed. "Why am I the only one in my family with the flu?"

"Everyone's had it in school," Jessica said consolingly. "Ms. Kantor was out on Monday and Tuesday. She sounds as bad as you."

Ms. Kantor was their fifth-grade classroom teacher.

"We're starting a new unit in science about astronomy," Jessica announced. She sounded excited. Astronomy was one of her favorite subjects.

Abby blew her nose again. At least they weren't studying germs. "What else are we doing?"

"In creative writing, Ms. Bunder had us write sonnets. We had a multiplication quiz and read a chapter of *Tuck Everlasting*. Ms. Kantor handed out astronomy fact sheets."

"I got a C– on my electromagnetic report," Abby groaned, "and now I'm missing astronomy. Not to mention multiplication quizzes and sonnets."

"Don't worry, you'll catch up," Jessica reassured her.

Abby closed her eyes. "Great," she muttered. "I can't wait."

"I asked Ms. Kantor for your assignments," Jessica said. "So you won't get too far behind. My mom and I will drop them off a little later."

"Thanks," Abby said. "I hope I can do them."

"Oh! I almost forgot!" Jessica cried. "Ms. Kantor announced that the fifth grade is having a science fair this year."

"Science fair?"

"We're doing it with Mrs. McMillan's class. The teachers are assigning partners tomorrow. And Ms. Kantor said we'll have a chance to get extra credit."

Abby suddenly felt exhausted. Too much was happening. She didn't want to think about science fairs and extra credit and partners with another class. She didn't want to think about astronomy units and bad grades and sonnets and homework assignments. She just wanted to sleep.

"I have to go," she croaked. "I can't talk anymore."

"Get better soon!" Jessica said.

When she woke up, it was dark and the smell of dinner filled the house. For the first time in days, Abby was hungry. She slowly got out of bed and put on her old blue bathrobe. She ran a brush through her tangled, snarly hair and tried to smile at her pale reflection in the mirror.

She *did* look like a ghost! A hideous, disheveled ghost! And a hungry one.

"You're out of bed! Are you feeling better?" her mother asked. Olivia Hayes wore the gray pin-striped suit that she put on for court appearances. Her hair was done up in a bun and she wore a gold and pearl necklace.

"I just got home," she said. "Your father told me you slept all day."

"Uh-huh," Abby said. Her throat didn't feel as sore and her limbs didn't ache as much as they had.

Her mother put her hand on Abby's forehead. "Your fever is gone. Are you coming down for dinner? Your father made roast chicken and potatoes."

"Yes," Abby said. "I'm starved."

"That's great!" Her mother smiled at her. "You're starting to get better."

Abby leaned against her mother. "I'm sick of being sick!"

"'This, too, will pass,'" her mother said, giving Abby a hug.

"*When* will it pass?" Abby asked. "I want to go back to school!"

Her mother shook her head. "Probably not until Monday."

"Awwwww," Abby said.

Her mother smiled. "I don't hear that very often." She hugged Abby again. "I'm going to make the salad for dinner. Why don't you wash up and come downstairs?"

Abby headed for the bathroom. Her walk was slow and shuffling. She felt like a patient in a hospital ward. In front of the mirror, she stared at her pale face, limp hair, and blinking eyes.

"You look awful," she told herself.

She washed her hands and splashed water on her chin and cheeks.

"What is wrong with this face?" she asked. "Find three problems and win a prize."

She squirted scented body lotion onto her arms and neck and face.

"Problem one, hollow cheeks," Abby said. "Problem two, circles under eyes. Problem three, cracked, dry lips. Where's my prize?"

She found Eva's raspberry kiwi lip gloss in a drawer. Pretending it was lipstick, Abby coated her lips. She pinched her cheeks to redden them.

She pulled on a strand of her hair. It was usually curly and wild and red. Today it was lifeless and dull and pale. Had the flu even drained the energy from her hair?

A pair of scissors lay on the shelf. She picked them up and snipped at the ends of a curl. It bounced back around her face.

"That's better," she said.

She clipped at it some more. Just an inch or two shorter was all she needed. And maybe she could cut the worst snarls instead of combing them out.

She wetted down her hair and shaped the sides, the front, and the top. She cut out a few snarls. Then she fluffed her hair with her fingertips and trimmed some more.

Abby smiled. She had never known she could cut

her own hair. It was easy. Why didn't she do this all the time?

"Dinner!" Alex yelled.

"Coming!" Abby cried hoarsely. "Just a minute."

She aimed the blow-dryer at her hair, scrunching the curls in her hand. In a minute, her hair was dry.

Abby stood back to survey the results in the bathroom mirror.

Her hair looked like someone had cut it with a jigsaw. It was uneven and raggedy. She hadn't trimmed and shaped, she had hacked and slashed.

It was the most awful haircut she had ever seen.

Chapter 2

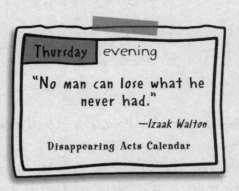

Thursday evening

"No man can lose what he never had."

—Izaak Walton

Disappearing Acts Calendar

<u>Not</u> true! I lost my hair AND my hair-cut. They're in the bathroom garbage pail nestled in with used Band-Aids, Q-Tips, and disposable razors.

<u>What I had (and lost)</u>:
A hairdo.

<u>What I have (and wish I could lose)</u>:
A scare-do.

Can't tape, glue, or paste my hair back together again! (I tried.)

(Now understand how Humpty-Dumpty felt.)

News Flash! Horrible Hair Hidden Under Hot Hat!

As Alex Hayes called her to dinner, Abby Hayes stared with dismay at her reflection in the mirror. Her hands strayed to her shorn locks. She tried in vain to force them into shape.

What would her family say when they saw her horrible haircut? They would make jokes, ask unpleasant questions, tease her, and shake their heads.

"Dinner!" Alex yelled again. "We're waiting for you!"

Abby plopped a towel on her head, then  a shower cap. Neither worked. She dashed into her bedroom, found a striped wool hat, and shoved it on her head.

A few straggling curls stuck out. She

tucked them into the hat. Then she went downstairs.

The entire Hayes family was sitting at the table when she came downstairs. Everyone looked at Abby as she took her place between Alex and Isabel.

The tragic ten-year-old held her breath. She was sure her mother or father would ask her to take off the hat at the table. Someone was bound to ask why she was wearing a wool hat to dinner in 75-degree weather.

Paul Hayes smiled. "Good to see you among the living again, Abby."

"Yeah," Abby mumbled. She pulled the hat down over her ears.

"Are you feeling chilled?" Olivia Hayes asked with a concerned frown. "Is your fever up again? You look flushed."

Eva jumped to her feet. "I'll get an afghan!"

"I'm okay," Abby said. She helped herself to a large piece of chicken and a baked potato.

"You're sure?" her mother said again.

"My head is a little cold, that's all," Abby muttered.

The Hayes family expressed concern and worry. Olivia Hayes said Abby could eat upstairs in her room. Isabel offered to serve her dinner in bed. Alex said he would read her a story.

Abby Hayes politely declined all offers of help. She pretended to be brave. She didn't pretend to be hungry. She ate two pieces of chicken and a whole baked potato with butter. She also drank a huge glass of milk.

When Abby went back to her room, she took the hat off. She was flushed and sweaty from wearing a wool hat on a warm evening. Her hair looked even worse than she remembered!

What will Abby Hayes do?

Stay tuned for further reports!

This is Abby again. (I wish it wasn't.)

I wish I was Natalie with short hair. I wish I was Jessica with long, straight hair. I even wish I was Brianna with perfect hair!

14

I wish I was anyone but me!

What I Look Like:
A lawn mower ran over
my head.
I cut my hair blindfolded.
The revenge of the
scissors!

Solutions (I hope):
1. Glue hat to head. (Too hot. Hair won't
grow right.)
2. Shave head. (Will look like newborn
baby or male wrestler.)
3. Buy wig. (It's not Halloween.)
4. Don't come out of room until hair
grows back. (Will miss spring and summer.)

I want my hair back! Now!!!

Later Thursday evening:

Jessica dropped off my homework. Alex
brought it upstairs. I was reading Tuck
Everlasting. It was pretty good. It was

helping me forget my problems when Mom
knocked on the door.

The Unkindest Cut: A Play with One Part
(down the middle of my head)
by Abby Hayes

Act I

Mom: Abby? Can I come in?

Abby is a ten-year-old girl recovering
from the flu. She is wearing purple paja-
mas. Her curly red hair has a ragged
appearance. At the sound of her mother's
voice, Abby grabs a wool hat with light-
ning speed.

Abby: Just a minute!

Mom is a lawyer and a mother of four.
She is carrying a shower cap and a pair
of scissors. A few stray red curls dangle
from her hand. As she enters the room, she
looks suspiciously at the wool hat on her
daughter's head.

Mom: Hi, Abby.

Abby tries to say something but her stomach is sinking.

She speaks directly to audience: Why do
stomachs sink? They aren't ships or boats.

She quickly recovers: Hi, Mom.

Mom: How are you feeling?

Abby (tries to look innocent): Congested, Mom. What's up?

Mom (directs a searching look at her daughter. Her eyes are like lighthouse beams or high-powered flashlights): I found these scissors and shower cap and this hair in the bathroom.

Abby: Really?

Mom: Mmm-hmmm.

Abby (puts on astonished expression): That's amazing.

Mom: Is that all you have to say?

Abby (nods): Yes.

Mom (points to the wool cap on her daughter's head): What's underneath that hat, Abby?

Abby (stomach sinking to the bottom of the ocean): Not much, Mom.

Mom: Take it off.

Abby slowly and reluctantly pulls the cap from her head.

Mom (stares): I can't believe this.

Abby says nothing.

Mom: Why did you try to cut it yourself? What were you thinking?

Abby: I looked awful!

Mom shakes her head. She sighs loudly.

Abby (despairingly): Now I look worse!

Mom: Maybe it's not as bad as it looks.

Abby: It is.

Mom: Let me see what I can do. (She
picks up hairbrush and begins brushing
daughter's hair.)

Abby: Don't bother.

Mom (stands back to check the results):
You're right. It _is_ as bad as it looks.

Abby: I _told_ you.

Mom (glances at scissors): Maybe I can
trim it a little.

Abby (suddenly hopeful): Can you even it out?

Mom: Of course I can. I have an objective eye.

Abby (again speaks directly to the audience): What is an objective eye? A legal
term that Mom uses in court? Or some
kind of grammar?

Snippets of hair fall to the floor as her
mother trims and clips.

Abby: All I want is a hairdo instead of a scare-do.

Mom: Next time, ask me for help. A shampoo and a hot bath would have made all the difference. It's normal to look awful after a week in bed.

Abby (nods): Okay, Mom. I'll remember that. Thanks for helping now.

Mom (hands her daughter the mirror): You're welcome.

As the act ends, Abby looks eagerly into the mirror.

Act II

The curtain rises. Abby Hayes, age ten, stares in horror at her face in the mirror.

Mom (apologetically): Sorry. I didn't improve it, did I?

Abby: Not much.

Abby (to the audience): My mother knows all about briefs, torts, and affidavits. She knows about running long distances, running a household, and serving on community boards. But she doesn't know anything about cutting hair!

(Despairingly) <u>Why</u> don't they teach that in law school?

Mom: Your sister Isabel did a good job of cutting my hair once.

Abby: NO!

Mom: Maybe she can give us some advice.

Mom exits room. Comes back with Isabel.

Isabel (picks up scissors): I know what to do.

Abby: <u>Don't!</u>

Isabel (puts down scissors): I don't want to cut it, anyway. It's hard to cut curly hair. Mom's is nice and straight. Yours is unpredictable.

Abby (sarcastic): Thanks, sis.

Enter Eva: Need some help?

Mom and Isabel: We're trying to figure out what to do with Abby's hair.

Eva (studies her younger sister): Forget it. It's hopeless.

Abby (very sarcastic): Thanks a <u>lot</u>.

Final Act

The curtain rises. Abby looks at herself

in the mirror. There is an expression of terror and deep despair on her face.

Her mother and sisters surround her. They sing their regrets in a chorus.

The curtain falls.

Backstage After the Play:

My hair looked like a battlefield. It looked like a football field after a scrimmage. It looked like a courtroom riot.

"Too many chefs spoil the 'do,'" my mother said sadly. "I made it worse."

"I thought that was impossible," I said.

My father came into the room. For a moment, he was speechless. "Is there a professional on the premises?" he finally asked.

"I'll make her an appointment first thing tomorrow morning," my mother said. She looked embarrassed.

"Hair today, gone tomorrow," my father joked.

I scowled at him. "That's so funny I forgot to laugh."

"By tomorrow, this will all be a memory," my mother promised. "Jeannie's the best in town. She'll give you a haircut that'll make you forget this one. I'll get you to her right after school."

I coughed and blew my nose to remind everyone how sick I was. "For your information, I am not going to school tomorrow!"

(Even if I wanted to go to school, I'd never show up with this haircut. I'd faint first. I'd run a fever. I'd develop a terrible lingering disease. I'd...)

Fortunately, I don't have to. I'm still weak from the flu. I will spend Friday drinking orange juice and trying to catch up on my homework. Dad will take me to get my hair cut later in the day.

Chapter 3

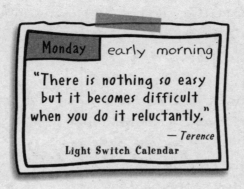

Monday | early morning

"There is nothing so easy
but it becomes difficult
when you do it reluctantly."
— *Terence*
Light Switch Calendar

<u>What should be easy:</u>
Getting up.
Brushing hair.
Walking to school.

All of these things are difficult because
I don't want to do them!

<u>Why they are difficult:</u>
I have to look at my hair in the mirror.
I have to walk outside with my hair.
I have to go to school with my hair.

<u>Why they are especially difficult:</u>

The haircutter is out of town until Thursday afternoon! She's the only one I trust to cut my hair.

I wonder if Ms. Kantor will let me wear a hat in class. (Probably not.)

Can I tape leaves onto my head and pretend I'm a tree? (Idea for science fair project.)

Or put a paper bag over my head and say I'm a walking sculpture? (Get extra credit in art.)

Abby walked onto the school playground with her best friends, Natalie and Jessica.

"There ought to be a haircut hospital," she said. "With ambulance service. Call 911 for hair emergencies."

"You'll be okay," Jessica said reassuringly. She was a tall girl with long, straight brown hair that she wore in a ponytail. "No one will notice."

"Oh, yeah?" Abby said.

Natalie adjusted the strap of her backpack. She

was a slight girl with short, dark hair who never paid much attention to her appearance. "Tell everyone you did it on purpose. Or that it was a side effect of the flu. Laugh it off."

"I should have shaved it off!" Abby cried. "And gone to school bald. Wait until Brianna sees it!"

Brianna was one of their classmates. She had perfect hair, dressed like a model, took French and acting lessons, and was always the best at everything.

"Don't worry about her," Jessica said.

"Today we meet with our partners for the science fair," Natalie said.

"I can't wait!" Jessica cried. "This is going to be so much fun!"

"Who did you get for partners?" Abby asked. She tugged on the cotton hat that Jessica had lent her. Before they had left for school, her friends had put barrettes and clips in her hair. It had improved the look a little.

"Sarah is my partner," Jessica said. "She's interested in ecology and the environment. We're going to study the effect of pollution on viewing stars at night."

"I got paired with Dylan and Amanda," Natalie said. "We went to the park this weekend and decided to grow crystals for our project."

"What should *I* do?" Abby asked her friends. "Study the structure of a hair molecule? Analyze the difference between curly and straight hair? Find out how fast hair grows after it's cut?"

"Get your mind off your hair, Abby," Jessica advised.

"My hair is on my mind," Abby said. "Get it?"

Her friends stared at her.

"That's the kind of bad joke my father loves," Abby explained.

The three girls walked up the stairs to the school. Their classmates greeted them.

"Spelling test today!" Mason yelled at them.

Abby shrugged. She had studied all the words over the weekend. Besides, spelling was easy. It was a lot easier than math. It was easier than science, too. She wouldn't need any extra credit in spelling.

Ahead of them, Brianna and Bethany were talking about their weekend. As usual, Brianna was the best-dressed girl in the fifth grade. She was wearing a short mirrored dress and chunky shoes. Her glossy dark hair was perfectly cut.

Bethany looked like the mirror image of her best friend. She was also wearing a short dress and chunky shoes. Her hair was blonde and braided with ribbons. She looked like Brianna, but she was a lot nicer — especially on her own.

"My hamster Blondie had babies this weekend," Bethany announced to the fifth graders around her. "Does anyone want one?"

Brianna frowned in irritation. "Is that all you think about?" she asked Bethany. "Hamsters?"

Bethany looked hurt. "They're so cute."

"Let's talk about *me* for a change," Brianna said. "This weekend I won a sailing race on the lake."

"I'd like a hamster," Natalie interrupted. "If my parents will let me have one."

"Ask them as soon as you can," Bethany said. "If I can't give them away, my mother said I'd have to bring them to the pet store."

"I came in way ahead of everyone else," Brianna continued. "Bethany! Are you listening?"

"Sure," Bethany said. "Yay, Brianna. You're the best."

Jessica rolled her eyes. "There they go again."

The three friends walked into their classroom together.

"Abby! You're back!" Ms. Kantor exclaimed. "It's good to have you in the classroom again. I hope you're feeling better."

Abby handed her teacher a written excuse and the makeup homework she had done over the weekend. "I'm better," she said.

"At least until I take my hat off," she added under her breath. Her heart began to thump. Ms. Kantor had a "no hats" rule. Any minute now, she'd ask Abby to take it off. Or maybe she wouldn't notice?

Abby sat down at her desk and took pencil and paper out of her backpack. Her classmates took their places around her.

The bell rang. Morning announcements began.

"Good morning," the principal, Ms. Yang, said over the loudspeaker. "All rise for the Pledge."

Abby stood up and put her right hand over her heart. "I pledge allegiance . . ." she recited.

"You forgot to take off your hat," Ms. Kantor whispered to her.

". . . to the flag . . ." Slowly Abby reached up to remove the cotton hat. She glanced around the room to see if anyone was watching.

". . . of the United States of America . . ."

Abby dropped the hat onto her desk and automatically repeated the words of the Pledge. Her face was hot — and no one had said a word! How was she going to stand it when everyone teased her?

". . . with liberty and justice for all," she finished. Liberty — that's what she would have once she got a proper haircut. She hoped Jeannie would do justice to her hair.

The class sat down.

Over the loudspeaker, a third grader started reading a poem about pigs.

Brianna nudged her. "What happened?" she whispered, pointing to Abby's head.

Abby groaned. "Family haircut," she whispered back.

"They're the worst," Brianna said. "Hair torture."

"Yes!" Abby agreed.

"I know about bad hair days," Brianna confessed.

"*You* do?"

"You can borrow my hair gel at recess," she offered. "It's the best."

"Wow. Th-th-thanks," Abby stammered. She had never expected Brianna to be sympathetic.

The announcements ended.

"We're going to get together with our science project partners in the library," Ms. Kantor announced. "I hope you all came up with ideas for projects this weekend."

A dozen hands shot into the air.

Ms. Kantor smiled. "We'll discuss them in a few minutes," she said. "If you don't have a partner yet, we'll give you one. Mrs. McMillan and I hope this will be the first of many projects our classes will work on together."

As Abby walked to the library, her classmates chattered excitedly about their projects. No one commented about her hair.

Abby hurried down the hallway to catch up with her friends.

"I'm going to grow molds," Mason announced loudly. He burped. "Kyle and I are going to have the most disgusting science project in the school."

"That's easy," Jessica said under her breath. "They're the two most disgusting boys in the school."

"I'm going to write a computer program," Zach said. "Tyler and I got paired with Daniel. He knows as much about computers as we do."

Abby was silent. She hadn't given any thought to her project because she didn't know who her partner might be. Abby hoped it was a girl who liked the same things she did. Someone who loved writing and Rollerblading and the color purple.

In the library, the students drifted into groups of two and three. Abby went up to Ms. Kantor.

"I know, Abby, you don't have a partner," Ms. Kantor said with a smile.

She looked down at a list of names. "Mrs. McMillan and I are hoping that you will learn new things about science and make a new friend, too."

"Sure, Ms. Kantor. My mother says you can never have enough friends."

"Let's see. Your partner will be Casey Hoffman, who just transferred from another school."

"Okay." Abby didn't know Casey Hoffman, but she'd be glad to show her the ropes.

"This project will be a part of your grade," Ms. Kantor explained. "You can earn extra credit for a difficult or elaborate project."

"Jessica told me."

Ms. Kantor gestured to Mrs. McMillan. "Send Casey over." She picked up her folder. "You two will get along well," she predicted.

Abby waited in front of a rack of paperback books. How did Ms. Kantor know that she would get along well with Casey? What if Casey was like Brianna? Or if she didn't like anything that Abby did? Or if —

"Did someone cut your hair with a lawn mower?" It was a boy Abby didn't know. He had dark eyes, dark hair, and ears that stuck out.

Abby had written the same thing in her journal just a day ago. It was one thing, however, to write it herself in the privacy of her room and another to hear a boy say it loudly in the middle of a crowded school library.

"No, they cut it with a nail scissors!" Abby retorted.

"In the dark?" he asked with a huge grin on his face.

"How'd you guess?" Abby asked.

He folded his arms across his chest. "High IQ."

"Does that stand for Idiotic Quotes?" Abby shot back at him. "Or Ignorant Questions?"

"Impossible Quizzes," the boy said.

"Ha, ha," Abby said. She glanced around the room. There was no sign of her partner.

"Don't you have a science fair project to work on?" she asked.

"Don't you?" he mimicked.

"I'm waiting for my partner," Abby said. "She'll be here any minute. You better go find yours."

"I know who my partner is," the boy said.

"Oh, yeah?" Abby said. "Why don't you go find him?" *Get lost,* she added silently. *Go bother someone else.*

"*Her,*" he corrected. "My partner is a girl." The grin on his face widened.

"So???"

Ms. Kantor hurried toward them. "Have you two begun work on your project yet? Do you need help?"

"Everything's great," the boy said.

"No, it's not!" Abby retorted.

"We've got plenty of ideas," the boy said.

"No, we don't," Abby said. "Ms. Kantor, I need to find my partn — "

She suddenly stopped. Why hadn't she put two and two together? Why hadn't she seen what — or who — was right in front of her nose?

"Good." Ms. Kantor consulted her list. "I won't worry about you. I know you'll both do just fine."

Abby turned to face the boy.

"You're — " The words dried up in her mouth.

The boy nodded. "I'm Casey Hoffman. I'm your science fair partner."

Chapter 4

Wednesday

"Two heads are better than one."

Troll and Monster Calendar

It depends which two!

<u>Head One:</u>

Abby Hayes. A bad haircut and a good mind. At least, it's a good mind for some things. I have good ideas for science fair projects (after consulting a lot of books in the library).

Examples:

1. How does water move through a leaf?

2. Do cats' eyes glow in the dark?

3. What causes dew?

<u>Head Two:</u>
Casey Hoffman. An ordinary haircut and an evil mind. Proof of evilness: constant jokes about my hair.
Example:
"You must be hair-brained!" Laughs. "Ha, ha, ha. Get it?"
Other proof of evilness: his science fair project ideas.
Examples (there are millions):
1. He wants to study different parts of the fingernail and toenail. (Exciting.)
2. He wants to test our reflexes. He throws cotton balls at my face, and everyone in the class watches me blink. (Forget it!)
3. He wants to breed fruit flies and maggots on decomposing bananas. (Ugh! Ugh! UGH!)
Final ultimate proof of evilness:
He calls me "Hayes." And pretends to sneeze when he

sees me. "I have Hayes fever," he says. "Ha, ha, ha. Get it?"

* * *

These two heads are not better than one. They cancel each other out. We spent the entire hour arguing. We have not decided on a science fair project.

If I don't do the science fair project, I'm going to get a really bad grade in science. If I do a last-minute science fair project, I won't get the extra credit that I need.

And it's all Casey's fault.

I hate him! I hate him! I <u>hate</u> him!

"Your hair doesn't look too bad today," Jessica commented. She twirled around on the swing. "Is it growing out already?"

"Brianna lent me her hair gel," Abby said. "That stuff really works. It glued down the sticking-out parts."

"*Brianna* lent you her hair gel?" Natalie repeated. "Are you serious?"

It was recess. The spring sun was hot. The three friends were on the swings, talking.

"She said it was the best," Abby said. She leaned back and looked up at the sky. "And she was right."

"You get it cut tomorrow," Jessica reminded her, twirling in the other direction.

"Jeannie better do a good job!" Abby sat up again. "I'm sick of barrettes, bows, and Brianna's gel. I like to brush my hair once in the morning and forget about it."

"How's your science fair project coming?" Natalie asked Abby.

"Ugh!" Abby groaned. "Casey is a case."

"Dylan is nice," Natalie said. "So is Amanda. She invited me to go swimming with her this weekend."

Jessica took a package of gum from her pocket. She unwrapped a piece and put it in her mouth. "Sarah and I are going to the library Friday after school."

"Does everyone like their partner except me?" Abby cried.

Natalie pointed to Bethany, who stood at the edge of the playground. She was watching her best friend Brianna. Brianna was laughing with Victoria, her partner from the other class.

"Bethany doesn't like *Brianna's* partner," Natalie said.

"That's different," Abby said. She began to pump

her legs. The swing rose into the air. "She doesn't have to work with her."

"Bethany looks really unhappy," Natalie said. "I feel sorry for her."

"That's what she gets for being friends with Brianna," Jessica said.

Brianna and Victoria shrieked, then grabbed each other's hands. A look of misery passed over Bethany's face.

Natalie waved at her. "Bethany! Come here!" she yelled. "I want to talk about Blondie's baby hamsters!"

"If that doesn't cheer Bethany up, nothing will," Abby said, skidding to a stop.

Bethany approached the three friends.

"Hi," she said. She sat down between Abby and Jessica.

"My parents said I can have a hamster," Natalie told her. "I just have to keep its cage clean and make sure it doesn't escape."

"Blondie was up all night on her wheel," Bethany said. "She kept waking me up. Are you sure you want a hamster?"

"Yes!" Natalie said.

"I'm constructing a maze for Blondie for the science fair," Bethany confided. Her eyes followed

Brianna and Victoria across the playground.

"Who's your partner?" Abby asked.

"Crystal," Bethany said.

"That name reminds me of a chandelier," Abby said. "Or something that breaks."

"Crystal is the kind of person who breaks things," Bethany said gloomily. "She's nice, but she's not much help."

Jessica jumped up. "There's Sarah!" She waved at a short, plump girl with curly brown hair who was kicking a soccer ball.

Sarah kicked the soccer ball in Jessica's direction. Jessica rushed to intercept it. The two girls passed the ball back and forth.

"They're good, aren't they?" Natalie said. She didn't like sports, although her parents kept trying to make her participate.

Abby felt a twinge of jealousy. She liked soccer, but she wasn't that good. And she wasn't interested in ecology or astronomy.

It was bad enough that she didn't like her science fair partner. It was even worse that her best friend liked hers so much.

"Aaaachooo! Aaaachooo!" The sound of loud, fake sneezing came from behind them.

The three girls turned around.

"Aaaa*chhoooo*!" Casey said.

"We don't want your germs," Abby said. "Go away."

"Awwwwww," Casey said.

"That means get *lost*," Abby said. "Understand?"

He grinned. "I thought you'd be nicer, Hayes."

"Hayes?" Natalie looked at Abby. "Is that what he calls you?"

Abby tried to shrug it off. She blushed furiously instead. Great. Now she was as red as her hair.

"I have an idea for our science project, Hayes." Casey stuck his hands in his pockets. "You're gonna like this one."

Abby glared at him. "If it involves throwing objects at my face or growing slimy molds, I won't do it."

"Picky, picky," Casey said. "How about extracting salt from seawater?"

"Boring."

Natalie nudged her. "That could be fun."

"No," Abby said.

"We could make a study of animal tracks."

Bethany nodded her head in agreement, but Abby ignored her.

"No," she said again.

"Why not?" Casey demanded.

"Because," Abby said.

There was a short silence.

"Do you have a better idea?" Casey said.

"We could experiment with natural dyes," Abby said after a moment. "My neighbor, Heather, uses onionskins and dried flowers to dye yarn."

"I'm not doing anything with yarn!" Casey said. "Knitting is for girls."

"Men used to knit for a living hundreds of years ago," Abby informed him. "Heather told me all about it."

"They don't do it today, Hayes."

"Stop calling me Hayes," Abby said. She looked to her friends for support. "We're never going to agree!"

Natalie jumped up. "I have an idea. I'll be the judge and figure out your project. Will you both accept my advice?"

Abby and Casey glanced at each other, then looked away.

"Okay, I guess," Abby said. It was better than fighting for the next three weeks.

Casey shrugged. "Why not? Hayes will squash all of *my* suggestions."

"No, I'll spinach them," Abby corrected.

Casey started to laugh.

"Why don't you study hamsters?" Bethany chirped. "They're a fascinating subject."

"No thanks," Abby said politely. Bethany's hamster did nothing but nibble, sleep, and scamper on a plastic wheel. She wasn't exactly a pet with personality.

"I've got it!" Natalie cried. "Why don't you put a rock collection together?"

"Rocks are my friends," Casey announced.

"He has them in his head," Abby murmured.

"You can go around to different places, like the quarry or the lake or the schoolyard, and find different rocks," Natalie explained. "Then you can display them with a report on where you found them and how they were formed."

"Do it," Bethany urged. "It's easy. It'll be fun."

"It's a good idea. If Hayes doesn't brain me with a boulder," Casey said.

Abby's friends looked at her expectantly.

She scuffed her toe in the gravel. She wouldn't have to speak to Casey until they had collected all the rocks. And they could start working now.

"Oh, all right," she said. "It's not very exciting. But I'll do it."

"Aaachooo!" Casey said. "Now that we've agreed on a science project, I better go take some medicine for my Hayes fever. Aaaaachooo!"

Bethany giggled.

"He's kind of cute," Natalie said as Casey walked away. "I think he likes you, Abby. I mean as a friend."

"Ugh! No way!" Abby cried. Casey was the worst boy she had ever met. He was worse than Zach, Tyler, and Mason combined. "I'll never be friends with *him*!"

Chapter 5

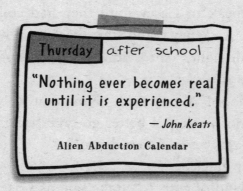

Thursday after school

"Nothing ever becomes real
until it is experienced."
— John Keats

Alien Abduction Calendar

Like the haircut I'm going to get in forty-
five minutes. I can't wait until I experience
it!

My Horrid Hayes Hair has been all too
real. I hope that Jeannie can fix it. My
mom says she's a genius with hair. It better be true!

Change of subject! I don't want to
think about my hair until it's time to get
it cut. I will write a play instead.

Playground Plays
by Abby Hayes

Abby sees Brianna and Bethany on the playground. She goes over to them. In her hand is a tube of Brianna's Best Hair Gel. She gives it to Brianna.

Abby: Thanks.

Brianna: It helps, doesn't it.

Abby: Yes. I'm getting my hair cut later today. Finally.

Brianna: Jacques cuts my hair.

Abby: Zhock?

Brianna: Jacques. Il est français. Tu comprends, n'est-ce pas?

Abby: Nest paws?

Brianna: It's French. So is Jacques. He's the best. He has an autographed picture of me on his wall. I'd never allow anyone else to cut my hair.

Bethany: Yay, Brianna.

Brianna preens and struts. Bethany cheers and admires. A fifth grader from Mrs. McMillan's class, Victoria, joins the group.

Victoria (excited): Brianna, I have, like, an awesome idea for our, like, science project, like, you'll never believe. It's, like, so cool. It's the best!

Brianna (excited): I asked my mother if you could come to dinner tonight. She said yes.

Victoria (excited): Awesome.

Bethany (not excited): Brianna, we were supposed to Rollerblade —

Victoria: She's, like, made other plans!

Brianna: I'm not in the mood to Rollerblade.

Victoria and Brianna link arms and walk away.

Abby (tries to cheer Bethany up): I, like, think, like, Victoria, is, like, not, like, that, like, awesome, you know?

Bethany doesn't smile.

Behind her, Casey Hoffman is making faces. Abby turns around and sees him.

Abby: You don't have a part in this play!

Casey: Awwwwww!

Abby: It's bad enough having to be your

science fair partner! Now you're showing up here!

Casey: Don't blow your stack, Hayes. Hayes stack. Get it?

Abby: Make like a needle and disappear.

Casey: Ha, ha, ha.

Abby signals the remaining actors, who exit offstage.

She writes "The End" in large, purple letters. Casey vanishes. She smiles and puts down her pen.

The Absolute, Final, Utter End

Dad just knocked on my door. He reminded me that in ten minutes he's driving me to Shear Delight for my haircut.

"I didn't forget!" I told him. "I've only been waiting for this appointment for an entire week. That's seven days, nine hours, and forty-two minutes."

"Okay, okay," Dad said. "I get the idea." He checked his watch. "Be downstairs in nine minutes and twenty-three seconds!"

* * *

I must stop writing. I must stop writing
now. I must put on my sneakers and take
all the barrettes out of my hair. I promise
to report back as soon as I get home from
Shear Delight!

<u>Thursday evening:</u>

<u>The Hair-raising Tale of a Trim</u>

   Jeannie, the hair-genius, whistled when she
saw me.
   "Wow," she said. "Your own mother did
this?!"
   "Yep," I said.

She led me over to the
sink and shampooed my
hair. Then she applied
conditioner that smelled
like bananas and straw-
berries.
   "My hair smells good
enough to eat," I said as she rinsed off
the conditioner.
   "It already looks like someone chewed on

it," Jeannie commented as she led me to a big leather chair.

I sat in front of a wall of mirrors. Jeannie pulled on the strands of wet hair. "Shall we go short?" she asked.

"No!" I cried. "I don't want to look like a boy."

"You won't," she promised me. She combed out my hair. "I'll give you a bob."

"What's that?"

"It'll be around your chin. Not too short. But not long, either. You've already cut a lot off."

"Okay," I said nervously. "As long as it looks better than now."

Jeannie laughed. "Don't worry about that!"

Curls of wet hair fell to the floor as Jeannie snipped and clipped.

"Why is it called a bob?" I asked. "Why not a steve or a jonathan or a zeke? Why would a haircut be named after a boy?"

"Don't know," Jeannie said. She spritzed my hair and trimmed some more.

"Do you have an objective eye?" I asked. "That's what my mother said before she started cutting."

"I have a diploma from beautician school." Jeannie scrunched my hair with her hands. "Let your hair air-dry and don't use a blow-dryer. Otherwise you'll wreck all your curls."

"I hate them!" I groaned.

"Your hair is gorgeous," Jeannie said. "It's to die for."

"It's to die from," I mumbled. "Especially this last week."

She handed me a mirror. "What do you think?"

"Okay." I didn't want to look.

"Just okay?" She gestured to my father. "Come here and take a look at her!"

"Wow!" my father said as he joined us.

Jeannie nodded in agreement.

"Cute," my father said, handing her some folded-up bills.

The other customers smiled. My face turned red. Only now I had less of my hair to match it.

Jeannie gave me samples of the straw-
berry-and-banana shampoo and conditioner.

"Stay away from those scissors!" she
warned as we left. "Don't let your mother
near them, either."

Dad took me out for ice cream. We
talked about rocks. He said Alex got a bag
of rocks for his birthday from his friend
Collin.

I didn't know that! (Is it possible to live
in the same house with siblings and miss
important facts about them?)

Note to self: Be extra nice to little
brother. Set table at dinner, even if it's his
turn. Don't complain when he hogs computer.
Pretend dumb cartoons are exciting.

Gently suggest that he lend me his rock
collection for my science fair project.

When I got home, I looked at myself in
the mirror.

"Bob" isn't too bad. (That's what I'm
going to call my haircut.) It's shorter than

I usually wear it, but it's not <u>too</u> short.
It curls around my face. Jeannie said I
don't have to fuss with it.

"Wash it and wear it," she said. "Just
like a T-shirt."

Jeannie did a good job. She <u>is</u> a hair-
cutting genius. I bet she's better than
Jacques. Will Brianna be jealous when she
sees "Bob" tomorrow?

The horrible haircut nightmare is <u>over</u>!
Hooray! Hooray! Run fingers lightly
through hair. Skip around bedroom. Call
friends! Arrange for group photograph.

Chapter 6

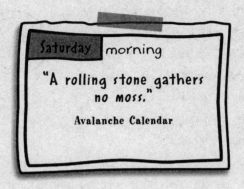

Saturday morning

"A rolling stone gathers no moss."

Avalanche Calendar

Neither does one in a drawer.

That's where Alex keeps his collection, in a blue pouch with a drawstring. None of his stones or rocks has gathered moss. (Why would they gather moss, anyway?)

He has pitted yellow rocks, green sparkly ones, blue-veined ones, clear pink, and shiny black ones. He says I can borrow them for my science fair project, as long as I take good care of them.

That should make things easy!

Except it doesn't.

Problem #1: We have to find most of the rocks ourselves. We have to keep a journal of where we find them, what plants and animals live nearby, and how they were formed.

It's not scientific if we only use Alex's collection and don't do any fieldwork. Or if we go to the Science Museum and buy the rocks.

That's what Ms. Kantor said.

Okay, I see her point. We're not supposed to <u>buy</u> a science project. Or have it given to us, ready-made.

But . . .

Problem #2: The rocks in my yard are boring. There's no calcite, fluorite, apatite, autunite, chlorite, hematite, molybdenite, orpiment, azurite, malachite, eclogite, kyanite, halite, pyrite, gypsum, or aphthitalite.

(Writing this is making me lose my apatite!)

There are no sapphires, rubies, diamonds,

basalt, tourmaline, amber, garnets, amethysts, zircon, turquoise, or topaz.

There isn't even any sandstone, limestone, or marble!

All I could find was gray rocks! They're all alike! (Did a colony of them settle in my neighborhood? Did they get rid of the different-looking rocks?) This is going to be the worst, most boring science exhibit in the world! I can't believe I agreed to do it.

"Rocks" by Abby Hayes and Casey Hoffman. Gray rock found at bottom of garden. Gray pebble from driveway. Gray stone under porch. Gray . . .

Aaaaaahhhhhhhhh!!!

Problem #3: Casey invited me to search for rocks today. Jessica and Natalie are getting together with _their_ partners. So are a lot of other people. He asked me in front of all my friends. I couldn't say no. He is coming to my house in only an hour. We are going to the park to look for rocks.

I have to spend the day with Casey Hoffman!

AAAAAAAAAAAAHHHHHHH! This

journal entry ends with a bloodcurdling scream.

"Let's walk toward the pond," Casey suggested. "I bet we find a lot of good stuff there."

"Okay," Abby said reluctantly. "I guess." She adjusted the straps of her backpack and hoisted it on her back.

The backpack held a notebook, pens, and guidebooks. It held a magnifying glass, labels, and plastic bags for sorting rocks. There was also a pocketknife and a microscope.

There was so much equipment, Abby wondered if the rocks would fit in!

"I hope this backpack is big enough," she said.

Alex pulled out a red nylon bag. "We can put lots of rocks in here."

"In Mom's laundry bag?" Abby exclaimed. "What are you thinking, Alex? It'll rip! It'll get filthy! Mom will be furious!"

"No, it won't rip! And Mom won't notice, anyway!" he protested. "Dad does most of the wash."

"Oh, yeah?" Abby said. "Besides, you won't be able to lug it home once it's full of rocks."

Alex's face fell.

"We can put our plant specimens in it," Casey suggested. "They'll be light. They won't ruin the bag. You'll be able to carry it home."

"Really?" Alex asked, brightening.

"Yep," Casey said. "I bet Hayes forgot to bring a bag for the plants. Didn't you, Hayes?" he said to Abby.

"We're collecting plants, too?" Abby asked irritably. "Aren't rocks enough?"

"Don't you want to get extra credit, Hayes?" Casey asked her.

"You need it, Abby!" Alex reminded her.

Abby scowled at the two of them. The afternoon had barely begun and already it was going in the wrong direction.

At first, it had seemed like a stroke of genius to invite Alex to join them.

"You have to protect me from Casey," Abby told Alex before they left. "You're my bodyguard."

"I'll be your buddy-guard," Alex said.

"Glare ferociously at Casey," Abby instructed him. "Don't let him call me Hayes. Don't let him tease me about my hair."

"I won't," Alex said. "Or we'll tease him right back."

"Two Hayes against one Hoffman," Abby said. "That'll even things out."

"Don't worry, Abby, I'll take care of you!" Alex promised.

"You're the greatest, Alex!"

Abby ran to her room and found a free ice-cream coupon that she had earned for doing extra chores. "This is for you," she said to her little brother. "You're a pal!"

But whose pal was he?

Since the moment they met, Alex followed Casey everywhere, listened to every word he spoke, watched every move he made.

Casey was extremely friendly to her little brother, too. He praised his ideas. He listened to Alex's endless conversation about robots. He told Alex stories about his family.

Casey and Alex were acting like best buddies instead of worst enemies.

It was infuriating! It was shocking! It was —

"You got a haircut, Hayes," Casey said to Abby as they crossed the park.

"Abby calls it 'Bob,' " Alex announced. "She cut

her hair when she was sick and made a mess out of it."

"Traitor," Abby muttered under her breath.

Casey nodded. "When I was little, I screamed so much when my mother tried to cut my hair that she had to sneak into my room when I was sleeping. She'd snip at it in the dark with blunt scissors," he said. "In the morning, my hair would stick out at weird angles."

"Ha, ha!" Alex yelled.

Abby gazed straight ahead.

"I think there should be a funny haircut contest," Casey said. "The winners could march in a parade."

"Uh-huh!" Alex agreed.

They turned onto a narrow path that led through the woods. From time to time, Casey stooped to pick up a rock that caught his eye.

"Watch out, Alex, that's poison ivy," Casey warned him. "That shiny stuff with three leaves."

"Have you ever had poison ivy?" Alex asked him.

"Yes, and it's no fun," Casey replied. "It itches like crazy. My older sister had it on her feet. She couldn't walk because of the blisters. My mother had to carry her around for a week."

"I won't put poison ivy in the plant bag!" Alex promised.

"You better not," Abby said. "That's all I need — poison ivy." What with bad haircuts, obnoxious science project partners, and traitorous brothers, she had all the problems lately that one fifth grader could handle.

"Look, a frog!" Casey pointed to a bullfrog poised on the edge of a rock.

Alex rushed toward it. With a splash, it disappeared into the water.

"I used to catch those little tree toads about the size of a thumbnail," Casey began telling Alex.

Abby tried not to listen. Listening to Casey Hoffman go on and on wasn't her idea of an exciting afternoon. Especially when Alex was hanging on his every word.

The three of them emerged from the woods. The sun was shining on the tall grasses by the pond. Birds darted back and forth. A few people strolled or sat at the edge of the water.

"A rock!" Alex cried. He picked up a large flat stone with a marbled surface.

"There are lots of them," Abby grumbled. She wished that she were home. "Big deal."

"Thanks, Alex. This is a real find." Casey examined the rock, then opened his backpack to put it away.

He took out a package of cookies. "Want one, Hayes?" he asked Abby.

"No thanks." Abby turned away.

Casey shrugged. "That means more for me and Alex. Right, Alex?"

"Right, Casey!" Alex shouted.

"Some buddy-guard," Abby muttered.

"I'm going to catch a frog," Alex announced, his mouth still full of cookies. He kicked off his shoes and waded barefoot into the pond.

"Stay close to the shore!" Abby warned him.

"Don't worry, Hayes, I'm a great swimmer," Casey said. He crossed his arms over his chest.

"Why do boys always brag?" Abby said.

Casey grinned. "Because it's true. Why do girls always worry about their hair?"

"I *don't* always worry about my hair!" Abby cried. "That's *not* true!"

"Don't blow your stack, Hayes."

"That wasn't funny the first time you said it."

"My jokes get better with age," Casey replied.

"*You* don't!" Abby retorted.

"Ha, ha, ha," Casey said.

"Shouldn't we be working on our science project?" Abby reminded him. "Why don't you go sketch a rock?"

Casey pulled out a notepad and a stick of charcoal. "Great idea, Hayes. I planned to sketch the natural habitats." He handed her some plastic bags. "You can sort your rocks into these."

"Gee, thanks," Abby said. "I already brought some."

Casey snapped his fingers. "Name three categories of rocks."

"Metamorphic, igneous, and sedimentary," Abby recited. She had studied them the night before.

"Just checking to see if you were on your toes."

"Oh, yeah? Name two kinds of igneous rocks!"

"Um . . ." Casey scratched his head. "Granite and . . ."

"Wrong!" Abby cried triumphantly. "Intrusive and extrusive."

"I got a frog!" Alex yelled, running toward them with cupped hands.

"Awesome," Casey said. "Let me see."

"Do you know the structure of the earth?" Abby asked Casey.

He shook his head. "No, I don't." He turned to Alex. "That's a baby peeper, Alex."

"Ha!" Abby said. "I do! There's the crust, the solid mantle, the molten outer core, the solid inner core . . ."

"Shhh!" Alex said. "You're scaring my frog."

"We have to keep ahead of the facts," Abby lectured Casey. "Otherwise we won't get a good grade."

"Later, Hayes," Casey said, taking the frog from Alex. "This is important."

"So is *this*!" Abby retorted.

"Ssshhhh!" Alex said again.

Abby marched over to the pond.

"I gave up a free ice-cream coupon for *this*?" she fumed. "I should have left Alex at home with his robots!"

She could have endured a few hours of teasing from Casey, she told herself. That would have been nothing. She could have teased him right back. But watching Alex become friends with Casey was the worst!

It wasn't fair! Alex was supposed to confide in *her*, admire *her*, want to be with *her* . . .

Was she jealous of Casey Hoffman?

No — of course she wasn't. Casey was jealous of

her. She had a great little brother like Alex, while he had an older sister dumb enough to walk in poison ivy barefoot.

Abby smiled. She picked up some rocks. She would fill her pack while Casey was admiring the baby peeper. She would label and classify the rocks. The faster she got done, the sooner the afternoon would be over. She would take Alex home. He would never see Casey again.

Chapter 7

Tuesday

"Those who do not complain are never pitied."

— Jane Austen

The Great Big Calendar of Sneezes

I complained all day Sunday. No one pitied me at all. Why not???????

<u>Pathetic Events in the House of Hayes:</u>

1. As we were leaving the park, Alex invited Casey to our house.
2. Casey said yes. He stayed for the afternoon.
3. Mom invited Casey for dinner.
4. He sat at the table right next to me.
5. My entire family liked him.
6. He watched a movie with us.

7. Dad <u>finally</u> drove him home at 9:00 p.m.

8. That adds up to eight whole hours of Casey Hoffman.

9. An overdose!!!! I have a bad case of too much Casey!

No one in my family pities me. No one attempts to understand my terrible ordeal. Not one single person. Not even the cat! Why not? Why not? Why not?

Mrs. McMillan's class and Ms. Kantor's class had gathered in the library to work on their science projects.

An excited buzz arose from the class. The students' materials were spread out over the tables. Victoria and Brianna were folding a pile of fashionable T-shirts. Crystal and Bethany argued about a hamster maze. Mason was blowing up balloons and popping them loudly. Jessica and Sarah discussed pollution. Natalie, Amanda, and Dylan examined the crystals they had grown.

Casey and Abby sorted through their rock collection. They had divided their collection into three sections: igneous, metamorphic, and sedimentary. They selected the best for display and threw out duplicates.

"How's 'Bob' today?" Casey teased as he compared two different specimens of sandstone. "Are you taking good care of him, Hayes?"

At the next table, Brianna looked up.

"Who's Bob?" she asked Abby. "Your boyfriend?"

"My haircut," Abby said. She picked up a polished piece of jasper and turned it over to examine it. It had come from Alex's collection.

Victoria frowned. "Like, why do you name your haircut?"

"Like, why not?" Abby glanced at Casey. He was grinning.

"That's a lot of T-shirts," Casey said to Victoria and Brianna. "Are you studying the science of shopping?"

"We have an even better idea," Brianna bragged. "We're comparing different brands of T-shirts. We have five categories: cost, appearance, durability, colorfastness, and shrinkage."

"Like, this is the coolest," Victoria said, holding

up an apple-green shirt. "I totally love this color, you know?"

"This one." Brianna held up a lace shirt. "If it shrinks in the wash, I'm going to buy another one. It's so totally cool."

"They need a Cool-o-Meter," Casey said under his breath.

If anyone but Casey had said it, Abby would have laughed. Instead she pointed to a piece of volcanic rock. "What's this?"

"That's from my sister Jamie. She got it in Hawaii."

"The sister with poison ivy?"

Casey nodded. "Look at this," he said. "I found rose quartz and fossils in my drawer. The fossils are from the lake."

"I'll write up the labels," Abby offered. She scribbled some notes on a piece of paper. "I'm also writing reports on how the three types of rocks are formed."

"Great, Hayes," Casey said. "With my pictures, we're bound to get a good grade. Wait until you see them. They'll knock your socks off!"

"I wish you'd knock off the bragging instead," Abby murmured.

Casey laughed. "You haven't seen my pictures. They'll change your mind!"

"Where do you, like, buy your socks?" Victoria asked Casey. "How, like, long before they, you know, get holes?"

"If you want to know about socks with holes, ask Alex," Casey said.

"Whose boyfriend is Alex?" Brianna demanded.

"He's in second grade," Casey said. "He's Abby's brother. And he has plenty of holes in his socks."

"His drawer is full of new ones," Abby explained quickly. She didn't want everyone to think that Alex went around with ripped clothing. "He just forgets to put them on."

"That sounds like Alex," Casey said.

"He's *my* little brother," Abby reminded him.

"You know Abby's family?" Brianna asked Casey.

Casey tossed a rock from one hand to another. "I had dinner with them on Saturday night."

"Oh," Brianna said. Her eyes widened. She glanced at Victoria.

"Alex invited him!" Abby said quickly.

"You don't need to hide it, Abby," Brianna said. "You should be proud of having a boyfriend."

"Yeah," Victoria breathed. "Like, I'd be telling *everyone*."

"He's *not* my boyfriend!" Abby cried. "He's not even a *friend*!"

Casey ducked his head.

"Who, like, cares?" Victoria said. "I mean, whether he is or isn't your friend or boyfriend, you know." She laughed.

"He's *not* my friend!" Abby repeated.

Casey looked away. His mouth curled down. He reached for the box of rocks and began to sort them.

Brianna and Victoria returned to comparing their T-shirts.

Her face flushed, Abby picked up a rock specimen and wrote a label for it. Then she labeled another.

"Class?" Ms. Kantor and Mrs. McMillan rang a bell at the desk to get everyone's attention.

"Start cleaning up your projects," they announced. "We're returning to our classrooms in ten minutes."

Casey emptied the rocks they didn't want into a large paper bag.

Abby sealed up the three boxes of sedimentary, igneous, and metamorphic rocks and their labels.

Neither of them spoke. Abby avoided Casey's eyes.

"Should I take these home?" she finally asked.

"Okay." He didn't look at her, either. "I'll get rid of the extras."

Mrs. McMillan rang the bell again. Without saying another word, Abby and Casey went to their separate classrooms.

Chapter 8

Wednesday

"I never apologize."
— *George Bernard Shaw*
Daily Excuse Calendar

When I quoted this to my family, they all disagreed!

Mom: Everyone makes mistakes. It's a sign of character to admit that you're wrong.

Eva: Not apologizing can ruin a friendship.

Alex: When someone hurts your feelings, it helps if they say "sorry."

Isabel: A little apology goes a long way.

Dad: "I'm sorry" are two of the most important words in the English language. Especially if they're sincere.

Abby: Is that true?

Entire family: YES!!!

I <u>don't</u> want to apologize to Casey Hoffman for anything!

But I think I'm going to have to. I've not only hurt his feelings, but I've done something much worse.

<u>News Report!</u>

At 3:15 p.m. on Tuesday, Abby Hayes, a fifth grader, walked home through the park. In her arms, she carried boxes of sedimentary, igneous, and metamorphic rocks. In her mind whirled furious thoughts about Casey Hoffman. She wished she had never met him. She wished she had another science partner. She wished —

"Abby! Abby!" It was Jessica, playing soccer with Sarah, the science partner she liked. "Come join us!" she called.

"We need a third player," Sarah added. She kicked the ball toward Abby.

Abby smiled.

"Just a minute!" she said. She carefully placed her rock collection under a tree. Then she ran into the field to join her friends.

The three girls played soccer for half an hour. Then —

We end the news report here.

The reporter doesn't want to report any more. The news is too painful to write. The reporter is too upset. Instead, she is going to whisper to her journal what happened next.

(I lost the rocks.)

I lost the rocks.

I lost the rocks!

I LOST THE ROCKS! (Okay, this is a shriek, not a whisper.)

Our science project is gone!

Dear Journal, you are probably wondering how I did something so dumb. Well, I played soccer with my friends, went to get a soda, and forgot all about the rocks. I went home, had dinner, started my home-work — and remembered that I had left them at the park. Dad drove me back. He said we'd find them where I'd left them — under the tree. We didn't. They weren't there — or anywhere else.

What happened to my rocks? Where did they go? Who took them? Will I ever get them back? What will I do?

We pause for a moment of silent scream-ing.

Help, help, HELP! The entire collection is gone. All the rocks we collected at the pond, in our backyards, and at school have disappeared. Alex's collection is gone and so are the rocks that Casey's sister Jamie lent us.

And what about the science fair? We <u>have</u> to complete a project! It's part of our grade, even without the extra credit.

Casey will be SOOOO angry! (How many apologies will I have to make? At least a billion. That probably won't be enough.)

What else can I do? <u>Think!</u>

<u>Make Excuses to Casey:</u>
   a) The rocks went on strike.
   b) A UFO took them to their leader.
   c) The rocks entered a time warp and are now in the Jurassic Era.
   d) They defected to another school.
   e) A wizard needed them for his experiments and I couldn't say no.

<u>Problems with Excuses:</u>
   (Obvious)

<u>Other Plans of Action:</u>
   a) Throw myself on Casey Hoffman's mercy.

b) Put together a second rock collection exactly like the first.

c) Pretend there never _was_ a rock collection.

d) Leave town for a year or two.

e) Blame it on the dog.

<u>Problems with Other Plans of Action:</u>

a) Hoffman will have no mercy on Hayes!

b) I can't _remember_ what was in the first rock collection.

c) Yeah, right.

d) Never mind.

e) What dog?

Even Better Plans:

Be practical. Think of a solution. Don't be afraid.

There is always an answer. That's what my mother says.

What is it? I need to know _NOW_!

Chapter 9

Thursday

"Leave no stone unturned."

— Euripides

Garden Tractor Calendar

We didn't.

Dad, Eva, Isabel, and I went to the park again last night to look for the rock collection.

We looked everywhere. Even in the water. Even in trees. Even in trash cans. We didn't find it.

We asked park employees if they had seen it. We asked Rollerbladers. We asked mothers and babies. We asked grandfathers and skateboarders.

We asked dog-walkers and kids with purple hair.

No one had seen the rock collection.

I asked Dad and twin genius sisters what to do.

"Tell Casey," they all said.

"Don't you have another answer?" I asked.

They didn't.

Why did I worry so much about my haircut? That was nothing compared to this! I'd rather go to school bald than tell Casey Hoffman the truth!

I might have to. Tell Casey Hoffman the truth, I mean.

(Maybe I should shave my head. . . . If I was bald, no one would remember the rock collection.)

Dad, Eva, and Isabel all promised not to say anything to Alex — for a while.

"You'll have to replace his collection," Dad said to me.

"Okay," I promised.

That'll be easy — especially compared to the rest of what I have to do.

Time is running out. My class is meeting his class this afternoon. Casey expects me to bring our project. What am I going to tell him? This is the worst moment of my life!

As Ms. Kantor's class filed down the hallway, Abby clutched her binder and rehearsed what she was going to say to Casey.

"I left it at home . . . We can work on it later . . . I don't know where it is."

That last one, at least, was true.

Abby groaned. She had had butterflies in her stomach all day. There were probably wasps, bees, and mosquitoes there, too. Even creative writing hadn't cheered her up. Her favorite subject with her favorite teacher had tortured her the way math usually did.

Ms. Bunder had asked the class to describe their favorite place and what it meant to them.

All Abby had been able to write was "My favorite place is anywhere but here." She had crumpled her paper into a ball and thrown it in the garbage.

Ms. Bunder had looked at her in surprise but didn't say anything. Abby didn't explain.

At recess, Abby had stayed in. She didn't want to encounter Casey Hoffman. Her friends went outside. Ms. Kantor talked with Ms. Yang, the principal. Abby stayed alone in the classroom.

Now, as the class walked to the library, Abby hoped to talk to her friends. But they were all engaged in other conversations.

Natalie was deep in a discussion of hamsters with Bethany.

Jessica was already in the library. She was looking up information on the Web. She and Sarah were planning an overnight trip for the weekend. They were going to observe the stars in the country *and* the city and see where they shone brightest.

Mason and Zach were talking about inventing a Burp-o-scope for an extra-credit science fair project.

"Let's rate burps like earthquakes!" Zach suggested.

"I'll be first to test it out." Mason burped loudly. "That's an eight on the Mason-Zach scale!" he shouted.

"Quiet!" Ms. Kantor warned.

Brianna was surrounded by a group of girls. She

was telling them how she had modeled for a cream-cheese commercial.

Abby wished she could turn into a block of cream cheese. Or even cottage cheese. As they got closer to the library, her heart began to thud violently. Her face flushed. Her stomach cramped. Maybe she was getting sick again?

She sat down in the nearest chair while her classmates hurried to meet their partners from the other class.

Brianna and Victoria greeted each other with loud cries. "It's so, like, great to see you!" Victoria cried. "It's been, like, hours since recess!"

"I have the best T-shirts," Brianna said. "I brought five more."

Natalie, Amanda, and Dylan gathered at a table and unpacked supplies.

Bethany hammered at the hamster maze. Her partner, Crystal, handed her the nails — though she dropped most of them.

"What's the matter?" Ms. Kantor asked Abby. "Why aren't you working on your project?"

"I'm waiting for Casey," Abby mumbled. "He's not here yet."

"Get going!" Ms. Kantor said. "The science fair is only a week away."

Abby took a deep breath. "Ms. Kantor, I lost it," she said. Her voice shook a little. "I lost my science fair project. I left it in the park and it disappeared."

Her teacher frowned. "That's too bad, Abby. But you'll still have to do it over."

"I can't!" Abby cried.

Ms. Kantor shook her head. "Then you'll have to start a new project. Unless you want a failing grade."

Tears came into Abby's eyes.

"You'll find some ideas in here!" Ms. Kantor pointed to a library shelf with a display of science titles. "You can do it if you get started now. You don't have a moment to lose!"

Abby slowly walked over to the books and began flipping through the pages. Some of the projects looked too complicated; others looked too boring. Besides, Casey would never like anything she liked.

If he had been obnoxious before, Casey was going to be *impossible* once he found out that she had lost their science project!

Abby took a deep breath. She wished she could fast-forward in time. She wished it was next year already.

"Hi, Hayes!"

"Hi." Abby darted a quick look at Casey's face. How should she begin? "Uh, hi," she said again.

"How's Bob?" Casey asked in a friendly way.

"Bob is wild," she answered. Maybe they could talk about her hair instead of the rock collection.

Casey grinned at her. "Glad to hear it. Where are we sitting?"

"Over there."

He went to the table and unpacked a set of drawings. "Come on, let's start. Where are the rocks?"

Abby's heart thudded. She couldn't sit down. "Those are nice drawings," she said.

"I knew you'd like them!" Casey said triumphantly. "Let's put them with the rocks and see how good they look together."

"Um, can we wait?" Abby said.

"Why?" Casey asked.

"Uh . . ." The room began to whirl around her. She put her hand on her forehead. Was she getting a fever? Was she going to faint?

"What's the matter?" Casey asked. "You okay?"

Abby took a breath. It was now or never.

"I lost the rocks," she whispered.

"You *what*?" Casey said.

"I lost the rocks!" she cried. "They're gone!"

Chapter 10

Thursday still

"The unexpected always happens."

-Swiss Watch Calendar

<u>YES!</u> (It's true.)

I told Casey the whole story. <u>Everything.</u> Once I began to talk, I couldn't stop. I told him about the soccer game, forgetting the rocks, going back to look for them twice, and realizing the collection was lost forever.
Finally, I was done. I stopped and looked at Casey.

I didn't expect to tell him everything. And I didn't expect his reaction, either.

* * *

He was frowning. His mouth was shut and he was gazing in the distance. He didn't say a word.

"If you're mad," Abby said, "I don't blame you at all. I'm so sorry."

Casey stared at Abby for a moment. Then he shook his head. "I can't believe you, Hayes."

"What do you mean?"

"You organized a search party and everything."

"So?"

"You should have called me!" Casey said. "I would have helped you."

Abby gaped at him. "You would have?"

"Sure."

"You wouldn't have been mad?"

"Naw. I lose things all the time. Socks, money, Rollerblades. It drives my mom crazy."

"This is worse than a sock. I lost your sister's volcanic rock from Hawaii," Abby pointed out. "Won't *she* be mad?"

Casey didn't say anything.

Abby shook her head. What was it with him? Didn't he get it? Didn't he understand what she had done?

"We have to redo our science project. That means starting all over again."

"We'll figure something out," he said. "Our two great brains will come up with an award-winning idea."

"Yeah, right," Abby said. "Two heads are better than one."

They exchanged glances.

"Have you told Alex?" Casey asked, after a moment. "Was he upset?"

"Not yet," Abby said. "I'm going to the Science Museum later today to replace his collection."

She patted her pocket. She had brought $18.76 to school. She hoped it was enough.

"I hope I can remember what was in the collection," she added. "I tried to make a list this morning, but — "

"I'll help you, Hayes," Casey offered.

"Thanks . . . Hoffman."

Casey and Abby looked at each other. Then they looked away.

He took out a piece of paper. "We better start thinking about what we're going to do next."

"Right," Abby agreed.

"More rocks?" Casey suggested.

Abby frowned. "How? We can't replace our collection in a couple of days! We'd have to collect it, sort it, label it . . ."

"Yeah . . ." Casey flipped through his drawings. "It's just a shame to lose all this work."

"I did a lot of work, too. I wrote up a report about how rocks are formed." Abby pulled out three typewritten pages.

"Maybe we can use our work in another project."

"Oh, yeah? *What?*" Abby demanded. "A demonstration of the rocks in my head? How to lose your rocks *and* your marbles at the same time?"

"That's pretty funny, Hayes."

"Ha, ha," Abby said. "I wish I was as good at coming up with projects as I am with jokes."

She glanced around the room. Everyone else was busy with their projects. They were making charts and graphs. They were building mazes and growing crystals. They were measuring, comparing, and observing.

Only she and Casey were back at square one.

"We better think of an easy project fast," Casey said. "Or we won't have one at all."

"Volcanoes?" Abby suggested.

"Two kids in my class are doing them. How about proving yawns are contagious?"

"Ho hum," Abby said. "How about making home-made perfumes?"

"That's a girl project, Hayes."

"Are we going to fight about this again, Hoffman?" Abby said. "We don't have time to argue."

"You're right," Casey agreed. "Let's write down our ideas on a piece of paper and then we'll choose the best one."

"Okay . . ." Abby agreed. She pulled out a fresh sheet of paper and her journal.

Ideas for Easy Science Fair Project:
1.
2.
3.
4.

Uh-oh! I can't think of anything! Casey is staring at his paper, too. What are we going to do? How will I ever get extra credit? Forget about extra credit. How will I get a passing grade?

Must stop worrying and start thinking!

Thoughts:

1. Casey was pretty nice about my losing the rocks.
2. He's not that bad.
3. I don't mind him calling me "Hayes."
4. He gets all my jokes.
5. He's . . .

Must stop thinking and start worrying!

More Ideas:
1. Show how —

Help! Mrs. McMillan and Ms. Kantor just told us to put away our work. It's time to go back to our classrooms.

Casey showed me his blank page. I showed him my empty page.

Zero plus zero equals zero. Will that be our science project? Show how nothing comes out of nothing?

No, that will be our grade if we don't figure out what we're doing soon!

Chapter 11

Thursday still

"Man is able to do what he
is unable to imagine."

— Rene Char

Flying Acrobat Calendar

So is Girl!

A few hours ago I would have been
unable to imagine going to the Science Museum with Casey Hoffman. Or having a
friendly conversation with him.

I did both those things — and more!

We went to the Museum Store and
bought a blue drawstring bag for Alex just
like his old one. Then we went over to
the rock display and filled it with rocks.
Casey helped me pick out the ones that
Alex had.

They weren't like the rocks I found in my backyard – gray and boring! They were clear, pink, rose, blue, black, green, yellow, purple, marbled, shiny, dull, heavy, light, flat, and round.

"Too bad we can't use these for our project," I said to Casey, as I picked up a photocopied sheet telling their names and where they were found.

"Ms. Kantor and Mrs. McMillan said we had to do fieldwork," he said.

"We _did_ fieldwork, didn't we?" I sighed. "But I lost it. Maybe we can do a scientific study about disappearance."

"Great idea, Hayes!" Casey cried. "Where do socks go? They're always disappearing. Where do coins and buttons go? What happens to all the things that are never found?"

"Like our rocks!" I said. "Maybe I could do a survey of lost objects."

"With charts and graphs!"

"We'll interview the whole neighborhood!" I gestured with my hand. "We'll use a tape recorder and take pictures and—"

Casey interrupted me. "There are only five days until the science fair."

Both of us fell silent.

"Another brilliant idea hits the dust," I said sadly.

"Sorry, Hayes," Casey said.

I put the drawstring bag on the counter and pulled out my money.

"That'll be $13.51," the woman at the cash register said as she counted the rocks I had put in the bag.

I handed her the money. There was $5.25 left.

"Wait a minute!" I raced back to the display, picked up a few more items, and returned to the register.

"These, too, please," I said to the woman.

She put my purchases in a bag and handed them to me. "Enjoy your rocks."

"I wish I could," I said.

"At least Alex will," Casey said.

<u>More Unimaginable Things That "Girl"</u>
<u>Was Able to Do:</u>
  Walk home with Casey Hoffman!
  (Thank goodness no one saw us.)
  Invite him into my house.
  (Yes, I did.)
  Show him my calendars!
  (This is for real! I'm not making this
up!)

  Casey left. Then Alex came home. I told
him what had happened.
  (His reaction was not "unexpected" like
Casey's.)
  "You lost my collection?" he yelled. "The
one that Collin gave me for my birthday?"
  "I'm sorry!" I said. "I didn't do it on
purpose!"
  Alex kept on yelling. "I told you to take
good care of it!"
  "I'm <u>sorry</u>!" I said again. "I bought you
a new one to replace it."
  "It's not the same." Alex folded his arms
across his chest and glared at me. "I'll
never forgive you, Abby."

I glared back. "It's exactly like the one that was lost."

"It can't be!" Alex insisted.

"Casey said so."

"Casey?" Alex's voice suddenly changed. "When did he see it?"

"He helped me pick out the rocks."

"Casey helped you?" Alex repeated. "He was here?"

I nodded.

"Why didn't you tell me he was coming over!" Alex cried. He was mad again.

"I didn't know!"

Alex gave me another look. "Show me the rocks," he ordered.

I handed him the blue pouch. He opened it up and took out the rocks. He examined each one of them. Then he put them back into the pouch.

"This is all right," he said. "It's close enough."

I breathed a sigh of relief. (Note: why not a cough of relief? Or a whisper of relief? Or a huff of relief?) Okay, I nearly choked with relief!

"When is Casey coming over again?" Alex demanded. "I want to see him!"

"This weekend. We have to figure out a new science project and do the whole thing in less than a week."

"Robots?" Alex suggested. "I'll help you both."

"No thanks." I picked up my journal. "Go away, Alex. I want to be alone."

"Tell Casey I like the rock collection."

"Casey, Casey, Casey!" I cried. "What _is_ it with him?"

Five minutes later. Alex is gone. I am left with many questions.

Question: Is "Casey" a magic word? Alex would not have accepted the new rock collection without it.

Saying "Casey" transformed my little brother from furious to curious.

(Will it work on other members of the Hayes family? Must try at soonest possible opportunity.)

Another question: Why does my little

brother like Casey Hoffman so much?

Alex acts like Casey is the
sun, the moon, and the stars.
All he wants to do is revolve
around him.

Casey is okay. He's not as
bad as I thought. He's even nice sometimes. Well, once in a while. I don't want
to get too friendly with Casey Hoffman.

Like my mother says, "This is strictly
business!"

As soon as we're done with our science
project, that's it! I'm not going to hang
around with Casey any longer than I have
to.

Imagine what my friends and classmates
would say if I became good friends with
a boy!

Brianna: Abby has a boyfriend.

Victoria: Abby has, like, a boyfriend, you
know.

Mason: Abby has a boyfriend. (Burps a

ten-and-a-half on the Mason-Zach scale.)

   Jessica: You have a <u>boyfriend</u>?

   Natalie: "Did you say <u>boy</u> friend?"

(This is getting boring. It wouldn't be boring if it actually happened, though. It would be <u>horrible!</u>)

No, no, <u>no</u>! It won't happen!

   After the science project is finished, I won't invite Casey to my house ever again. I won't show him my calendars. I won't ask him to help me pick out rocks for Alex.

   I will spend my free time with Jessica and Natalie. And Bethany, too (if she stops talking so much about hamsters). We will play soccer together, have sleepovers, and talk about Brianna.

   I will say hello to Casey in hallways and at recess. I will joke with him. Once in a while I might even throw a ball to him. But that's <u>it</u>!

   Another question: Why is it so awful for

a girl to be friends with a boy? (This has nothing to do with Casey. Really!)

Suppose a girl and boy just like each other. As friends only. Why does everyone have to tease them?

I want to know!!!

One final question: Why am I writing so much about a boy????

Chapter 12

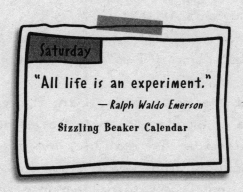

Saturday

"All life is an experiment."
— *Ralph Waldo Emerson*

Sizzling Beaker Calendar

Then it ought to be easy to figure out a science fair project!

It *is* easy to find a project if you look in the library. Casey and I took out six books of science experiments. There were <u>hundreds</u> of projects! We wrote down a list of our favorites:

1. Make a battery out of a lemon. (Then take a ride in your lemon mobile.)
2. Model how people imagined the universe in

the past and present. (People used to think the world was flat!)

3. Show how first-, second-, and third-class levers work. (This project will give you a lift.)

4. Find the parts of a bean. (Easy!)

5. Use a blender to show how igneous rocks are made. In real life, they're made from volcanoes and lava. Then show how pressure and layers turn them into sedimentary rock. (This experiment <u>rocks</u>! Ha, ha, ha. It really does.)

Casey found it. He pointed out that if we do this experiment, we can use our research, too!

<u>Hooray!</u> Hooray! Hooray! We started last night because it takes a couple of days for the "rocks" to form.

All we had to do was blend a bunch of construction paper in the blender with water and glue.

Then we strained the water and put our rocks on newspaper to dry. It will take only a couple of days.

We'll combine our new experiment with the old report and drawings. I bet Ms. Kantor and Mrs. McMillan will like it. Maybe I'll even get a good grade in science!

Abby dribbled the basketball down the driveway, stopped, and threw it at the basket.

The ball bounced off the rim.

"You need more follow-through," Eva said. "Like this." She picked up the ball and swished it into the basket.

Abby frowned and tried again. The ball ricocheted off the backboard. "I just can't get it," she complained.

"Try again," Eva encouraged her. She effortlessly made another basket, then passed the ball to Abby.

Abby threw the ball. It wobbled on the rim, then plunged into the hoop.

"Basket!" Abby cried. "I did it!"

"Way to go!" Eva said. She checked her watch. "I've got to get ready for softball practice now. Keep it up, Abby."

Eva hurried into the house. Abby's next shot didn't even hit the basketball hoop. Nor did the next.

"I'm not keeping it up," Abby muttered to herself.

Maybe Eva was her lucky charm. Maybe her athletic ability rubbed off on Abby. Unfortunately, it disappeared when Eva did.

The ball rolled into the grass. Abby didn't run after it.

She sat down on the back steps. Eva had softball practice; Isabel was at a play rehearsal; Alex was playing with a friend. Her mother was shopping and her father was in his home office.

She went into the house to get the phone. It seemed like weeks since she had seen Jessica outside of school.

"Is this Jessica? Hi, it's Abby."

"Hi." Jessica was laughing. "Just a minute." She covered the receiver with her hand. Then she came back on the line. "What's up?"

"Do you want to Rollerblade in the park?" Abby asked.

"Sarah's here," Jessica said. "We're putting the finishing touches on our report."

"Maybe afterward?" Abby suggested.

There was a pause.

"We're having a sleepover," Jessica said. "So I can't."

"Oh." Abby took a breath. "Well, have a good time."

"Thanks," Jessica said.

Sarah said something that Abby couldn't make out.

"Gotta go now!" Jessica said. "See you!"

Abby hung up the phone. She dialed again. "Hello? Is Natalie there?"

"Natalie!" her father called.

Abby waited.

"Natalie!" he called again. "Just a minute," he said to Abby. "I think she's in her room." He put down the phone.

Abby stared at a spiderweb on the ceiling. She heard Natalie's father going up the stairs and then coming back down again.

"Natalie is at Bethany's. She'll be back after dinner."

"Okay, thanks," Abby said. "You can tell her I called."

She sat with the phone in her lap. No reason to

call Bethany. She was with Natalie. Her closest friends were all busy. Now what could she do?

Call Casey? No. She couldn't. He was a boy.

But who else was there? Brianna?

"I must be crazy," she muttered to herself. "Or truly desperate. But at least she's a girl." She dialed Brianna's number.

"Hi, Abby," Brianna said. She sounded friendly.

"Want to Rollerblade in the park?" Abby asked.

"I'd love to," Brianna said. "But Victoria is here. We're going shopping. Want to join us?"

"Sure," Abby said. The words were out of her mouth before she could think about them. "Where?"

"At the mall. My mom can pick you up in half an hour."

"I'll ask my dad." She put down the phone and ran up the stairs. Then she ran back down.

"He said yes," Abby said to Brianna.

"Awesome," Brianna said. "Bring your credit card."

"I don't have one," Abby said.

"You don't have charge accounts?" Brianna asked impatiently. "How about a debit card?"

"Um, no. I'll bring my allowance."

"Victoria and I are going on a spree," Brianna said. "We're buying earrings, purses, and colored lip gloss."

"If I empty my penny jar, I'll have enough money for a chocolate pretzel," Abby said. She said good-bye and hung up the phone.

"I *must* be crazy," she said to herself. "Crazy, crazy, crazy."

Was going shopping with Brianna and Victoria *really* better than spending the afternoon alone? Or with Casey? Why had he been so nice about losing the rocks? It was much easier to hate him!

"Let's go in that store," Victoria said. "It's got, like, the most totally awesome face glitter. It's, like, the best."

"They've got cool things," Brianna agreed.

Abby tagged behind the two girls. They had been in the mall only fifteen minutes and already Brianna and Victoria had bought bracelets, anklets, and hair ornaments.

Brianna picked up a plastic purse with tubes of lip gloss inside. "Aren't these cute?"

Victoria made a face. "They're, like, for little kids."

"What do you think?" Brianna asked Abby.

Abby shrugged. "I'm not a purse person. Purse-son. Get it?" She made a mental note to say that to Casey. He'd think it was funny.

Brianna and Victoria didn't.

"These purses are cute," Brianna insisted.

"Like, okay. Don't, like, get all upset and, like, strange about it."

"I'm going to buy one," Brianna said. "I'll start a new fad."

"Like, who cares?" Victoria said nastily.

Brianna tossed her hair over her shoulder. "I'm number one! I take French lessons, act in commercials, ride horses, and sing onstage! *Moi, je parle français. Je suis très belle!*"

"Bell?" Victoria sneered. "Dingdong!"

"I'm a star!" Brianna cried. "I'm the most popular girl in the fifth grade."

"*I* am the most popular," Victoria said. "I mean, it's *me*."

"*You?*" Brianna retorted. "I don't think so!"

Victoria turned red. "You're so, like, you know, like, I mean, so, so, *like* — " she sputtered.

Suddenly she turned to Abby. "You decide!" she said. "Which of us is the most popular?"

"Um . . ." Abby scrambled to think of the right thing to say. If she chose one over the other, she was in trouble. If she said nothing, she was in trouble. Whatever she did, she was doomed.

"Can't you both be the most popular?" she asked.

"No!!" they yelled in unison.

"Or take turns?" Abby suggested.

"This isn't nursery school," Brianna said impatiently.

"Like, you can't expect us to share," Victoria snapped. "It's so, like, babyish."

"So who is it?" Brianna said. "Me or Victoria?"

Abby glanced at the clock on the wall. Forty-five minutes before Brianna's mom showed up. "Um," she said again.

"Well?" Victoria demanded. "We're waiting for your answer."

Abby took a breath. She felt as if she were trapped in a jar with two wasps. How could she keep them from stinging her?

"This is too important for just one person to decide," she finally said. "You need to ask more people!"

Brianna raised her arms skyward. "The people shall speak!"

"Everyone in the school should, like, vote on it," Victoria agreed.

"We'll hire an independent polling company."

"Or, like, a private investigator."

Abby edged toward the door. "I'm going to get a pretzel," she told them. "I'll be back in fifteen minutes."

"Don't, like, get lost or anything," Victoria told her.

"My mother hates to wait!" Brianna warned.

Abby found a bench outside the store, then pulled out her journal and began to write.

Phew! That was close! Good thing I thought of telling them that one person shouldn't make such an "important" decision.

Good thing there's a pretzel shop nearby.

Good thing they're so busy discussing the popularity contest, they don't care if I leave!

Who is worse? Brianna or Victoria?

Compared to Victoria, Brianna is nice.
Compared to Brianna, Victoria is modest.
Compared with Casey, they're both awful.
Even though they're both girls.

This afternoon of shopping will go down
in history as the "Mall Maul." I will
make the Hayes Book of World Records as
"Only Known Lone Survivor of Brianna-
Victoria Shopping Spree." (I hope I survive.
There are still twenty-eight minutes and fifteen seconds left.)

How many arguments will Brianna and
Victoria have in the next half hour? (hundreds)

How many bags of jewelry, makeup, and
clothing will they buy? (dozens)

How many times will Victoria say, "like,
you know?" (billions)

How many times will Abby wish she had invited Casey Hoffman to her house? (no comment)

An afternoon with Casey would have
been a breeze!

Why a breeze? Why not a zephyr, gentle wind, or a draft?

Okay, an afternoon with Casey Hoffman would have been a zephyr! (He would think that's funny.)

This afternoon with Brianna and Victoria is a tornado, a typhoon, and a monsoon. (They wouldn't think that's funny!)

Only twenty-five minutes and twelve seconds left.

I am killing time. Why kill time? Why not pass it, like a car on a highway? I'd like to zoom ahead at eighty miles an hour to tonight.

Uh-oh. Here come Victoria and Brianna. They are smiling and laughing. They are friends again. They have six new bags of "cool stuff."

Chapter 13

Sunday

"The next day is never so good as the day before."

— Publius Syrus

Daily Grind Calendar

Wrong! Today was <u>much</u> better than yesterday!

Today I invited Casey over. (All my friends were <u>still</u> busy! Jessica was at Sarah's. Natalie was with her family. Bethany was at Brianna's.)

It was fun having Casey here. Especially after spending the afternoon with Brianna and Victoria.

I don't know which was worse, their arguments or their agreements!

* * *

<u>Their arguments:</u>
(You know about them!)

<u>Their agreements:</u>
Brianna: Where did you get those awesome earrings?
Victoria: Like, your shirt is so totally cool.
Brianna: It's from Paris.
Victoria: So are my earrings! EEEeeeee!
Brianna: EEEEeeee!

I was so glad to see Casey, I gave him a present.

Casey: What are these?
Me: A fossil and a piece of rose quartz.
Casey: I know, but —
Me (interrupting): I bought them at the Science Museum. Didn't you guess?
Casey: No.
Me: To replace the ones I lost.
Casey: You didn't have to —
Me: Yes, I did.
Casey: Well . . . thanks, Hayes.

* * *

We worked some more on our science project. Our igneous rocks had dried, so we took two of them and made sedimentary rocks.

Then we wrote a report on what we did. Casey drew pictures of the blender and our ingredients. I mounted the new report and the old one on poster board. Casey tacked up his new drawing and his old on another piece of poster board.

It looked pretty good when we got finished. It looked like something that might get us a good grade. It might even get us extra credit.

Casey and I stood back to admire it.

Then I got my idea.

Chapter 14

Wednesday

"The future you shall know
when it has come; before
then, forget it."
— *Aeschylus*
Crystal Ball Calendar

Aeschylus wrote this in 458 B.C. All of his future is now past! Everyone has forgotten it.

My future is still ahead of me. And I <u>can't</u> forget it!

The science fair is tonight. Casey and I are going to set up our exhibit today in school. So will everyone else.

My whole family is coming to see the science fair.

Alex is excited because Casey will be there.

I am excited because the project is <u>finally</u> done!

And because I added a surprise to it. No one knows. I haven't told Casey. I haven't told my friends or family.

What will they think? What will Ms. Kantor think? What will Mrs. McMillan think? Will we get a good grade? Will we get extra credit? Will we get a prize?

My "surprise" isn't exactly scientific. It adds something to the project, though. And that's all the hint I'm going to give you, journal!

The Hayes family van pulled into a parking space behind the school. All around them, parents and students were getting out of cars.

"There's Natalie!" Abby cried. She rolled down the window and called to her friend.

Natalie was carrying a plate of cookies. "Hi, Abby!" she yelled.

Her father was right behind her. He turned to wave to Abby's parents.

Paul Hayes turned off the engine and opened the

car door. "There's quite a crowd here tonight," he commented.

"Don't forget you have to take me to the high school in twenty minutes," Eva reminded him. "I have a lacrosse game."

"And I have a Drama Club meeting," Isabel added.

Abby's mother sighed. "We're all so busy. I have a board meeting. But I still have plenty of time to see Abby's exhibit."

She gave her daughter a quick hug.

"I've already seen Abby's exhibit," Isabel grumbled. "I don't know why Eva and I have to come."

"You might be surprised!" Abby told her older sister. She picked up a grocery bag. Inside were two bottles of apple juice and some cups. Ms. Kantor had asked the students to bring refreshments.

"How?" Isabel asked. "Did you change the poster-board color?"

"You'll see," Abby said.

"We're a family," Olivia Hayes pointed out. She reached inside the car for her sweater. "It's important for us to support one another."

"There's Casey!" Alex cried. He sprinted down the sidewalk after him.

"Alex supports Casey," Eva said drily.

The rest of the Hayes family walked up to the school.

"Welcome to the Lancaster Elementary fifth-grade science fair." The principal, Ms. Yang, stood in the entranceway to greet the families and students.

"How's high school?" she asked Isabel and Eva.

"Not bad," the twins answered in unison. "Pretty good." They looked at each other and burst out laughing.

"It's a twin thing," Abby explained. Her sisters sometimes said the same thing at the same time.

"Did your older sisters help you with your science project?" Ms. Yang asked Abby.

"No, my younger brother did." She looked around for Alex, but he had disappeared. Casey was nowhere in sight, either.

The gym, where they had set up the exhibits, was packed. There were exploding volcanoes, animal mazes, levers and pulleys, and electrical circuits that lit up when you connected them correctly. There were parents and students and brothers and sisters. There were teachers and aunts and grandparents. Ms. Kantor rushed around with a camera, taking pictures of everyone.

"Hi!" Abby said to all her friends. "Hi!"

Her project was displayed on a table in the middle of the gym. Casey stood in front of it, explaining to parents and other students how he and Abby had made the rocks in a blender. Alex stood next to him, listening to every word.

"There you are, Hayes," Casey said. "I — "

"You missed it, Abby!" Alex interrupted. "The mayor was here! He looked at your project!"

"What was the mayor doing here?" Abby asked.

"He came to see me," Brianna bragged. "My cousin works for him."

At the table next to them, Brianna and Victoria had arranged half a dozen T-shirts. They had charts and graphs ranking each one. Each shirt was color-coded. On the graphs, each was represented by a different color gel pen.

"Our project is the coolest," Brianna bragged. "The mayor said we applied science to fashion."

Victoria looked annoyed. "My cousin who, like, owns a factory is coming, too. Doesn't your aunt work in his mail room?"

"Only because she wants to," Brianna said. "My aunt could get a job anywhere. She's the best."

"It must run in the family," Casey muttered.

"Someone has to do a scientific study of the 'B' gene," Abby whispered back.

"Abby!" Bethany waved to her from across the room. "Come say hello to Blondie!"

Abby threaded her way through the crowd. Bethany and Crystal's table was surrounded with curious onlookers. They were watching Blondie, Bethany's beloved hamster, scoot down the passageways in search of food.

"She's so intelligent," Bethany cooed.

Crystal bumped into the table. Their report fell on the floor. "Sorry!" she said.

"Good thing I brought extra tape," Bethany said.

"Sorry!" Crystal said as she dropped the report a second time.

Bethany rolled her eyes.

"Gotta go back," Abby told them. "Casey's all alone — except for Alex."

Casey hadn't said a word about the surprise yet. She wondered if he had noticed it.

"Hey, Hayes," Casey said. He was leafing through Abby's report on rocks. He put it down and smiled at her.

"Where's Alex?" Abby asked.

"He went off with Isabel. Your parents were just here. They'll be back. I — " he began.

"There's Ms. Bunder!" Abby cried. The creative writing teacher was dressed in black pants and a blue silk top. She wore sandals and had on a silver necklace.

Standing next to her was a tall bearded man in blue jeans and a T-shirt.

"Does Ms. Bunder have a boyfriend?" Abby wondered out loud. "She never said anything about him in class!"

Casey shrugged. His class didn't have creative writing with Ms. Bunder. "I wanted to — " he began again.

"I'll be right back!" Abby rushed off to say hello to her favorite teacher.

Ms. Bunder was talking to Zach's parents. She smiled at Abby, who waited for a break in the conversation. More parents approached.

"I'll catch you later," she said to Abby.

Disappointed, Abby headed back to her table. She wanted to tell Ms. Bunder about the surprise. Well, she'd show her later. Ms. Bunder would like it!

"*Finally*, Hayes!" Casey exclaimed. He looked grumpy. "You're leaving me all alone here!"

"Sorry," Abby said. "I *had* to say hi to Ms. Bunder."

"I just wanted — " Casey began.

"Jessica!" Abby cried. She waved wildly to her best friend. "I haven't seen your project! And I haven't seen Natalie's, either!"

"You haven't seen *ours*," Casey muttered.

"I won't be long — promise!" Abby said.

As she hurried toward Jessica's table, her mother emerged from the crowd.

"Abby!" she cried. "Your father and I have been looking for you."

"'I'm going to see Jessica's project," Abby said. "She studied the effects of pollution on viewing the night sky."

Her mother took her arm. "That sounds wonderful, but Eva, Isabel, and I have to leave soon," she said. "Let's go back to your table. I want you to show us *your* project."

The entire Hayes family had converged around the project table.

"You're back," Casey said in disbelief. "The posse must have rounded you up."

"It did," Abby said. "Sorry I — " She stopped in the middle of her sentence. Her mother was examining their homemade rocks.

"Casey and I made those in the blender, Mom."

Olivia Hayes looked startled. "I suppose your father said it was okay."

"I did," Paul Hayes said.

Abby's mother sighed. "I'll count my blessings. At least it wasn't our new food processor."

"These are great drawings of natural habitats," Isabel said to Casey.

"The report is good, too," Eva said.

"Casey and Abby did the *best* project!" Alex said proudly.

"Sshhhh!" Abby held a finger to her lips. "Don't let Brianna know!"

"Why not?" Eva said. "It's good to be competitive." She glanced at her watch. "Speaking of competitive, we have to leave soon. I don't want to be late for the game."

"Just a minute," Paul Hayes said. "I haven't finished looking at everything." He picked up another report. "What's this?" He turned the page. "'A Sizzling Scientific Surprise. A Tale of Two Projects,'" he read. "By Abby Hayes."

"Is this part of the science project?" Olivia Hayes asked her daughter.

"Well, uh, not really, but sort of — " Abby stopped. She was starting to sound like Victoria.

Isabel leaned over her father's shoulder. "Is this the surprise, Abby?"

"Uh, yeah, I guess so," Abby said, her face hot. She glanced at Casey. "I, uh, well — "

Paul Hayes handed the paper to his wife. "Read this," he said.

<u>A Sizzling Scientific Surprise! A Tale of Two Projects!</u>
by Abby Hayes

Something mysterious happened on the way to the science fair.

Abby Hayes and Casey Hoffman had assembled a rock collection from local and faraway sources. They had labeled their rocks and prepared detailed reports and drawings.

They had completed their work for the science fair — or so they thought.

* * *

Then the entire rock collection disappeared one afternoon while Abby played soccer with Jessica and Sarah.

A search party was assembled. Members of the Hayes family scoured the park. They queried every person they met. They followed every lead.

No rock collection appeared.

Using scientific logic, Abby concluded that the collection was "lost, stolen, or strayed."

Its whereabouts remain a mystery, even today.

A period of scientific inquiry followed. Casey and Abby still had the report and drawings.

Using the scientific method, they examined their choices. Assemble another rock collection? Throw out everything and start anew? Or build on their work for a new science project?

They chose the third. It was the most logical. Casey found the perfect project. They made igneous rocks in the blender.

They wrote up a new report, but kept the old one, too.

Conclusion: Two projects can be better than one!
Abby and Casey learned about rocks.
They also learned about mistakes, discovery, and starting over again.

"Great job," Olivia Hayes said. "I'm so proud of you."

Paul Hayes gave his daughter a hug. "Terrific, honey."

"Is that all you have to say?" Abby asked, disappointed. Parents always said things like "great" and "terrific" and "proud."

"It's true!" her father insisted.

"Don't let failure stop you," Eva added. "That's how to have a winning team." She pointed to her watch again. "Dad, it's time to go!"

"Drama Club always starts late," Isabel said. "But I need to be there early. Good work, Abby."

"I helped a lot!" Alex said.

"Yes, you did," Casey agreed.

"You both did a wonderful job," Abby's parents said once more. "Abby, we'll pick you up in an hour."

The Hayes family left the gym.

Abby and Casey straightened out the exhibit.

"I want to tell you — " Casey began again, when Ms. Kantor and Mrs. McMillan appeared at their table.

Chapter 15

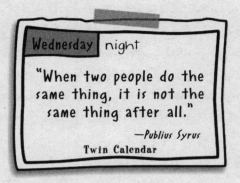

Wednesday night

"When two people do the same thing, it is not the same thing after all."

—*Publius Syrus*
Twin Calendar

Example:

Ms. Kantor and Mrs. McMillan gave us an "A" on our rock project!

Hooray, Hooray! <u>Hooray</u>!!!!

Even though they did the same thing, it <u>wasn't</u> the same thing.

Ms. Kantor said: "I think these two deserve extra credit. Look, they did two projects and Abby wrote this wonderful 'Sizzling Scientific Surprise.'"

Mrs. McMillan said, "Abby wrote the 'Sizzling Scientific Surprise,' not Casey. That's what makes this project really special. Only Abby should get the extra credit."

Thinking fast, I said, "But Casey did just as much work as me. We divided it up. He did the drawings and experiments. I was the project writer."

Ms. Kantor smiled at me.

"That's very persuasive," Mrs. McMillan said. "When you put it that way, it makes sense."

"So you'll give us both extra credit?" I said.

Mrs. McMillan picked up the blender rocks. She glanced at Casey's drawings and my reports one more time. "Yes."

"I think they deserve it," Ms. Kantor said.

Casey and I high-fived each other.

"Hey, thanks, Hayes," Casey said after they left. "You stuck up for me."

"Better than being stuck-up," I joked.

We both glanced in Brianna and Victoria's direction. The teachers were talking to them.

Brianna was arguing with Ms. Kantor. "An A+ is the only mark I'll accept," she said.

"Like, we bought all these T-shirts and gel pens," Victoria said. "We deserve an A+ for the coolest project in the fifth grade. We spent more money than, like, anyone else."

"This is about science, not money," Ms. Kantor said.

"When you're a teacher, you can give yourself all the A+'s you want," Mrs. McMillan said. "For now, you're getting a B."

"B?" Victoria said.

"B!" Brianna shrieked.

Off the Mark
A play by Abby Hayes

Place: you know where
Time: you know when
Cast of Characters: you know who

Brianna: B is for best, isn't it?
Victoria (annoyed): Casey and Abby got,

like, an A for a bunch of rocks!

Brianna: They weren't even real rocks! Just a bunch of mushed-up paper!

Victoria: Like, our project was so much more real.

Enter Bethany with hamster in her arms.

Brianna: What did you get?

Bethany: B+! That's the best mark I've ever gotten in science. (Kisses hamster.) Thanks, Blondie!

Brianna (dramatically): B+???? Truth and justice are dead!

Bethany (holding hamster out to Brianna and Victoria): Want to pet her?

Victoria: Eeeeuuu. Nasty. Get it away from me.

Bethany: You're hurting Blondie's feelings.

Victoria: Hamsters smell. Their eyes are, like, red.

Bethany: Blondie is listening!

Enter Natalie.

Natalie: We got an A on our project!! Hooray!

Brianna (sinks back onto a chair): They got an A. We got a B.

Victoria: Do you have to tell, like, everyone? Shut up, already!

The curtain falls. The play is over. So is
the science fair.

I asked Casey if he liked my "Sizzling
Scientific Surprise."
Casey said yes. (He had been trying to
tell me all evening.)
"It tied together our two projects," he
said. "It made them work together. It de-
scribed how we worked together."
"I wish they had given out prizes!" I
cried.
"We'd have gotten the Surprise Prize,"
Casey said.

Maybe Ms. Kantor will give it to us tomorrow? (It's never too late to give a Surprise Prize!) No, probably not.
Extra credit and an A are enough for
now. . .
Casey and I wandered outside. The PTA
was selling ice cream by the playground.

"Ice cream!" I cried.

Casey pulled some dollar bills out of his pocket. "I'll treat you. My mom said I should. She said it was nice of your parents to let us ruin your blender."

"We didn't ruin it. I washed it out right away," I said. "The container got stained blue, that's all. I don't think anyone will notice."

"Probably not," Casey said. "What kind of ice cream do you want?"

"Cherry chocolate chip. One scoop."

"Is that all, Hayes?" Casey asked. "Two scoops are better than one."

"If you say so, Hoffman," I replied.

One last word . . .

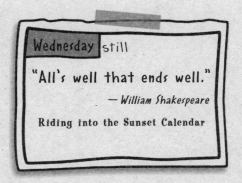

Wednesday still

"All's well that ends well."

— William Shakespeare

Riding into the Sunset Calendar

Ha, ha, ha, ha! Surprised you, didn't I?
I bet you didn't expect a quote at the <u>end</u>
of a journal entry!

Welcome to a world where magic is real and friendship is everything.